Stories by Bob Page

Edited by Lindsey Nelson

Illustrated by Keary Ingrum Jr.

Copyright 2015

Manic Me

The windshield began to spider web out from where I was kicking it in. I kicked it some more. Then I jumped off the hood of the truck, clicked my heels, did a cartwheel, and opened both doors to the cab as wide as they could go to let the volume rage on a most furious punk song. A crowd was starting to appear around me and my graffitied up bank-owned B2500 pickup that barely had 4,500 miles on it. I ran and danced through the ogling normals, doing cannon balls and body slams on the concrete path to the sound of machine gun drums. I ran behind the people and through the people doing more cartwheels; some folks were clapping, some were watching in fear, others knew I was just another freak on the strip, but I had my whole heart into it. Yes, I was the star of this show, the one and only Bob! Traffic started jamming up in front of...

"THE PARIS HOTEL AND CASINO IN BEEEAAAUTIFUL! LAS VEGAS, NEVADA! WHERE YOU AND YOUR FAMILY CAN WATCH BOB! BOB! BOB! AND MORE BOB! HE'S GOT SPILLS. HE CAN GIVE YOU CHILLS! HE'S GOT BLOODY KNEES AND SHREDDED CLOTHES WITH HIS OWN WRITING ON THEM! HE'S AMAZING! AMAZING! AMAZING! WATCH AS HE FINISHES OFF THE WINDSHIELD OF HIS

FINAL ARCH ENEMY, HIS BANK-OWNED TRUCK...THEE ANTI-CHRIST!" *End game show announcing voice in your head, please.* (Crowd goes wild.)

After that it was time for my very special grand finale. I ran sixty feet in front of my brand-new mess. Faced it. Made and an imitation of a charging bull and then went for it at full speed. I ran as fast as I could. I took off four feet in front of the truck. I flew over the hood and went elbow and head first into what was left of my windshield. It was a glorious end to a perfect performance! I had won. I caved in and had slayed the safety-glassed devil. It was still held together, but just barely. It was indented with the shape of my upper body and head. No worries, nothing could detract from my victory. I wiped the glass and blood from my face, got up, and stood on the roof of the cab. I took a bow and only one person clapped. I was on cloud nine.

Who was the clapper? It was an older, lonely, damn-gorgeous Greek lady. A...MILF, if I ever saw one. (Though I wasn't sure if she had any kids. We kind of had a language barrier.) Anyway, she thought I was a god amongst the street performers in the area. I saw her and ran back to the truck to turn the volume down. She followed and I introduced myself, shaking her hand; she smiled and laughed a good, genuine laugh, wiping my face with a tissue. I asked if she would like to go somewhere to hang out; she smiled and said yes. I asked her where we should go and she said we should go back to her room at the Flamingo. I cut myself again dusting off the thousands of glass shards on the passenger seat. She, for some reason, got in and we tried to find parking at the Flamingo.

We couldn't find parking in her hotel's garage. So we parked at another. As we walked back, we talked and played charades with each other. While we played this game, she pointed to a tattoo on her upper right arm and asked, "Know who?" I nodded and answered, "Sure, that's my man, Alexander the Great! From Macedonia." She shook her head laughing and thought it exciting that I knew who the guy was (though he was about all I knew of ancient Greece). When we arrived to her room she invited me in and we continued getting to "know" one another. In our conversation, she'd mentioned that the next day she was going to spend $300 on a rock climbing class at a place called Red Rocks, Nevada. I told her "Ah, don't even waste your money on that! Gamble it. I have this! I've got years of experience and all of my climbing gear in the truck. I'll teach you tomorrow." Then she was so happy with me, she ran and jumped on me. We began kissing with a passion I have never kissed a lover with since.

You see, the reason I had the rock climbing gear in the car was because I was going to pawn or sell it so I could by a cheap guitar for my new homeless friend that I had picked up at a famous book store in Palmdale, CA, just a few days before. We made the 200-mile trip out to Vegas with just $25 dollars on us. This guy played guitar like a million of your favorite guitar heroes rolled into one, but he was also probably a heroin addict, so he lacked ambition. He smelled really bad too! Anyway, I had a business plan. We were both going to stand on a corner on the strip and he would play guitar and I would sing, and in doing so MAKE A FORTUNE! We would take that money and gamble it in such a way, that our earnings would parlay. I would be his manager and take 60% of the money because I had a truck. He would counter my enthusiasm with "Bob. I am a classically trained studio musician. I WILL NOT PLAY ON A FUCKING STREET CORNER! This is crazy! Why did I come? We need to get back to the Antelope Valley!" He'd shake his fist at me with tears in his eyes and stuff, but it was all in good fun, because I was a genius. I was the son of god!

Back in the hotel room my kissing buddy said she was going to go downstairs to the gym and workout and that I should shower and nap. I told her "OKAY!" As she was walking out into the hallway, I grabbed her by the waist and pulled her back in the room, kissing her wildly again. Then she pushed me away giggling, exited the room and went down the hallway with a bounce in her step. I certainly had a bounce in my step. I had a bounce in my brain! I could have really used a nap. At this time I'd probably been up for forty eight hours straight with only three hours of rest before then, but I was still on fire! I showered, had a nap of about thirty minutes and, then BOOM, I was ready again!

The first thing my homeless amigo and I did in Vegas was run out of gas inside the parking lot of the Luxor. The second thing I did was get 86'd from the Luxor after trying to bum cigarettes and then smoking used butts out of the ash trays there. Hotel management did not like that. The third thing I did was go pan handle for gas funding. I was no liar, I actually was out of gas. My friend decided to sleep in the truck, missing all of the action. Later on, I would discover that honest pawn shops do not except used climbing gear (some kind of liability issue), even so, I eventually made enough money for gas and cheap hotel rooms. So Homeless and I (of course I was essentially homeless too at this point, but since I'd rather not use his real name I'll stick with the derogatory one) stayed at a no-name place across from Circus Circus.

You see, panhandling might seem easy and it can be, but only if you do not have pride and self-esteem. Once you kick these attributes to the curb, it can free up a whole bunch of things one wasn't previously able to do in public, like talking to thy self, moving one's appendages with no apparent reason sporadically, and busting out into song and dance at unforeseen times and places in front of anyone and everyone. What did it matter to the Universe what any of us did under its microscope? Just us humans living in a human world doing human things. Could the Universe really pick out a free radical like me from the rest? Does the Universe really care if one of the little humans ran amuck murdering, stealing, and rampaging? Not that I did any of the murdering, in all likely hood from space (if we can be seen or even thought about) this all looks like chaos. Us humans living in a human world doing silly human things: building cities, forging empires, lighting firecrackers and nuclear bombs, billions of us over and over through time, living, dying, suffering, loving, and enjoying. Not one of those things matter to the Universe. So what! If I was a bit off and not shy, strangers gave me money and I gave them crazy.

***

Location: The Flamingo's Gym on the main floor. Camera #5,552. Picks up a white Caucasian male about six feet in height and around two hundred pounds. Twenty to twenty-five years of age. Subject is blond. Wearing a white T-shirt with a bunch of writing on it and blue jeans.

Security earpieces blare: Attention! Units responding to the main floor gym. Subject appears to be deranged. Please use caution!

Camera #5,552 shows the crazy get behind a female patron on a treadmill and bust a jig. He then proceeds to jump on the same treadmill as the lady and start running behind her. The idiot's feet go out beneath him and he face plants into the machine's conveyer belt, which deposits him on the gym room floor. The single white female did not fall or get hurt. She seems, though, to be upset. Security has the man detained and is escorting him downstairs. PD is on the way.

LVPD Officer #1: Where is your ID? What does "Pleased to inspire minds otherwise Deemed Useless by society" mean? What's with all this writing on your shirt?

LVPD Officer #2: Why do you have all these cigarette burns on your arms? Mr. Page do you believe you're a danger to yourself and others?

LVPD Officer #1: That innocent women that you freaked out, said that she doesn't know you. Why do you insist that you two were hanging out? Listen man. We are not going to view the cameras to verify your story. That would take too long. Calm down brother! I think you are lying to us, sir. We will not find your wallet in her room! She is refusing to let us in. You know she is crying right now? She's scared of you and of us. For fuck's sake, she can barely speak English! What the fuck!

LVPD Officer #2: Listen Bob, security radioed back that they did find your wallet in her room and it took a while but she confirmed your story. Bob we don't feel like we can just let you go; we need to have a doctor look at you before we can. We feel that you might be a danger to yourself and others. Even though, for the circumstances, you seem like a decent guy, we have to place you on what we call, here in Nevada, a Legal 2000.

On the way to the E.R for evaluation, I struck up a conversation in a manic sense that made sense to me. I told the EMT-P (I was being transferred by ambulance after I promised LVPD Officer #2 I would not runaway from the crew) that I, at one time, had worked for the same company as he. I also told him that if he wasn't careful he could end up with the same kind of future as me, but that was all right because "Nothing really matters, sir." On and on, I told my plans to total strangers about how "I am going to become a king to the vapid, mediocre monkeys and lead them and inspire them with my FREE WILL! Only I have free will. They will have to follow me or die!" (Yes, follow me or die. I may use that as an ad campaign someday) I'd also tell 'em all "I serve god...I serve me."

Anyway, I'm sure it wasn't much of a conversation. The whole time. At this time. I could not sit still. I had to move something or shake something. If it wasn't my feet, it was my hands and arms; if it wasn't that, I had to rock from side to side. (I can't really explain the feeling now, as this was almost sixteen years ago, but I had the sense that I had to GO! GO! GO! every second of every minute of every hour!). Well we arrived at the hospital so "we" could find out what sort of drugs I was on. I insisted that I was not on drugs, but if I was, it must have "been that fucker that gave me his hamburger. That bastard!"

So while I was staying in the emergency room at one of the hospitals in Las Vegas, I, of course, made another scene, as was par for my course at this time. You see, there was this dragon lady of a nurse who, from the outside, appeared to be a princess, but really came off like a fire-breathing reptile of yester year. She wanted my pee and I kept refusing to pee in her collection cup. We argued about this for an hour or more. Her saying, "You have to pee sometime, you know? And I always collect!" and me screaming back at her "NEVER LADY, YOU WILL NEVER HAVE MY PEE! MY GOLDEN SHOWERS ARE FOR ANOTHER! FUCK OFF BITCH!" Tit for tat, back and forth. I'm sure the other staff and patients were getting upset with the situation. I don't know why she insisted on arguing with me, after all I was INSANE! I didn't know what her problem was. (Was she a nutty squirrel too?) Well, in the end of our ridiculously overt melee, Dragon Lady won out and I was cleverly sedated with something and she had my piss. When I awoke, it was the next day. I was in restraints and I had a catheter up my male appendage. I finally sat still. ER staff had told me that I was going to be sent for another kind of evaluation in another facility down the road. My test results came back negative for any kind of illegal substance and, on departure, Dragon Lady gave me a hug and called me a "sweetheart."

* * *

"Yeah, I'll take a blond and one ginger, please. Oh, you don't have any red heads? Well, whatever. Just make sure they don't have rabies or something, got it? Thanks!"

"ALL RIGHT BOYS AND GIRLS, THE PARTY WILL START IN EXACTLY ONE HOUR!" I yelled out to a handful of other inmates or patients or what they called us crazies in the mad house. Then with phone book in hand, I got on the phone and called the nursing station to threaten them with this little number: "My dad works on a state of the art nuclear bomber. If you bastards don't let me out in time for the strippers, I'm going to have him send a bomber to bomb me the hell outta this shithole you call a workplace! You understand? You imbeciles."

The nurse responded, "Mr. Page, if you don't get off the patient phones we are going to have to put you in the Quiet Room, sir. Please, hang up the phone, sir."

Me, "You may scare the other soulless captives with your empty threats lady, but you won't scare me! I'm hanging up only because I have other business to attend to, bitch."

After that, one of the patient phones rang. "Hello," I answered. A female voice said, "Hey, we're outside you son of a bitch! WE BOTH HAD TO DRIVE FROM ACROSS TOWN! YOU BETTER PAY US! I can't believe you called us from inside a psycho ward."

I told her to hold on and yelled out, "HEY, EVERYONE, THE STRIPPERS ARE HERE! THEY'RE WAITING AT THE FRONT DOOR!" I glared with hate at the nursing station and screamed, "AND YOU BETTER FUCKING LET THEM IN! THEY ARE WORKING GIRLS AND THEY NEED THEIR MONEY!"

Then I got back on the phone and the woman told me "I hope you die in there for this and then burn in hell! I flew in from Florida..." and then the line went dead.

I left the phone dangling and started pacing up and down the common area, cursing loudly at the nurses for about an hour before other staff arrived. I ran back to the phones and dialed 911. The operator asked "911, what is your emergency?" I frantically answered "Yeah, I have been kidnapped and I am being held hostage at this place somewhere in Las Vegas. I need you guys to come and arrest these people and get me out of... " The phone went dead on me and a group of staff, about seven deep, were closing in on me in a half circle and I was backed against a wall. I busted through them and ran around the nursing station through the hallway, running and jumping, going left then going right, again and again. I taunted the staff members over and over as I ran around the facility like Daffy Duck and just as cartoonish, until they got a hold of me and tried to get me on the floor. The insidious devils had done this before and through subterfuge shanked me with a needle to the thigh...soon after, I was out.

Sedation would keep me mellow for a while until the mania would slowly start in again. So I was able to stay calm enough to form a viable escape plan. I knew that my plan would take me about a week to complete and that I'd be in full-blown Hyperville when I was to pull it off.

When one first arrives to the loony bin, staff will take your shoe laces so you won't strangle someone or hang yourself or something similar. My plan involved socks (a lot of them) and running fast. I needed socks because my shoes, absent of laces, were too loose for my feet. The goal was to somehow collect enough socks to make a run for it. This took time as I had to barter with the other patients. Trading cigarettes, meal items, or just promising folks that I'd shut up for a period of time for a trade. I also told staff that I lost a pair and they gave me two pairs. I actually had a few plans to leave. One was trying to act sane in front of the doc and be let out, but that was impossible at this time. Another was to cause a distraction with a riot, but nobody else was having it. (This was hard because everyone of us had different things going on with them: schizophrenia, depression, retardation, people just staring at walls, people just walking into walls, homeless people, and me with my Hitler bi-polar mania in full swing. Nobody was on the same level, my rebellion had no united front). This orchestrate landed me in the padded sedation room again. I visited three times during my stay. My one construct that did work was this...

A patient was not allowed to loiter within ten feet of the locked buzz-in doors. I would be waiting twenty feet away when it was my time to go and one slow elderly staff member was to come in. I knew I could cover that twenty feet in a second—I *would* cover it in a second. I also had a ton of socks on and my boots fit. I was ready to run.

When it was time for the old lady's shift (she was a counselor or something) and I saw that she was coming through the first set of double doors, I kneeled down like a sprinter waiting for the crack of a pistol and then 3...2...1...BUZZZZZZ. I was down the main stretch! I must have freaked her something awful and I kinda felt bad. I was two hundred pounds and six feet tall, she was 4'11" and maybe 100 pounds. I'm sure she must have uttered "Goodness young man" as I peeled out of there and I said, "Pardon me young lady. I'll just squeeze by ya here. THANKS!"

I jetted out of there and the run was on! They had a security guard that was on duty and he pursued, but he had no heart (maybe his laces were loose). He also had no stomach for running into the heavy, fast traffic of one-hell-of-a-busy Las Vegas street, blindly letting Lady Luck take care of one's safe passage. Yes. He had no heart. He followed me slowly out onto a side street from a way's back only after he crossed the street in a legal manner. I slowed up and let him catch up. Then I start throwing rocks in his direction even though I knew he was well out of range. He had no taste for that and I never saw him again. I was free.

Where does crazy go in Vegas after escaping from a mental institution? Why back to The Strip, of course! It was a five- or six-mile walk back. I stopped at an exotic dance club that featured male talent and applied for a dancing position (even though I was about twenty-five pounds overweight and had torn clothing with gibberish all over it, was balding, and was missing one or two showers...I still had my confidence!) The staff there had taken me with a lot of salt and thought it had been fun that I had stopped by—they even let me audition!

Once back on the strip, I was famished. I had had a long day! So I walked into a busy fast food place and asked the staff for a water cup, then I turned from the service counter and at the top of my lungs announced to fifty or so patrons, "Excuse me, fine ladies and gentlemen. Can I have your attention? I am extremely hungry and I was wondering if I may beseech you? NOT! For work in which I will NOT do. And NOT! For money which I of course will squander! But with the utmost honesty, may I implore your conscience and BEG from you, YOUR sympathies. Please help a starving man with the aid of one or two sandwiches!" I was then pelted with three hamburgers from three different directions. This is how I would stay fed through all of this and it worked every...single...time.

***

Here, for now, is where I am going to leave this particular reflection. This rumination springs in me pain, laughter, and a wistful sense that I will never again experience such freedom, even if that freedom was only residing in my mind.

Long story short: I had just quit working on an ambulance as an EMT in Southern California. I had left with no notice in the middle of a night shift. It wasn't even a stressful shift, but I was STRESSED OUT! Maybe I had post-traumatic stress disorder, I don't know. All I knew at the time was that I had a hard time doing the most basic of things. I would "freeze" up just taking vitals or trying to splint simple sprains, getting a person into C-Spine for shipping, completing paper work, or even briefing ER staff. I'd just start crying for no real, outward reason. However, inside, I'd have this tremendous pressure in my head as if it was going to explode and an unexplainable paralyzing fear—I wanted out of my own skin. I'd be left in the back of a unit, a complete and total useless, frazzled moron.

I had a close associate advise me that maybe I should take some of my mother's serotonin reuptake inhibitors that she was not using at the time. These meds were the ones with the unhappy squares on TV that after they popped some happy pills, you know, they became...happy, and would bounce. Those ones. I took 150mg of them a day for about two weeks and I only noticed that I'd have to pee out of my butt and that my head felt like I was having to think through a heavy layer of fog.

So, now, drum roll please...thump...pound...thump...that is when I decided to stop taking these pills cold turkey. That was a mistake and my three-month ride into what the doctors would call Bi-Polar Mania began! I, at first, felt great, like I was beginning to think clearly. Then I thought I had above normal intelligence. Then I felt like I was the smartest goddamn person ever to have human brains. Then I thought I was omniscient. Then I thought that I was god and god had a name—and that name was Bob! Things went on and on. Night and day. Twenty-four seven for three months. Things just like the above story. I could not sleep, or I'd only need eight hours of sleep for an entire week, and that would be enough to conquer whatever. It is hard to remember every stunt I pulled during this long, horrible episode. There were just too many stunts! Like a pugilist in a bout with sanity. I fought through the nonsense trying beat in sense and after I had won, I was still fighting. For one hundred days!

I imagine the girl from Greece went back to Greece. I imagine the homeless man went back to the AV and then back to Los Angeles. I abandoned him in Vegas. Like I said, I imagine I do not know. My parents came to pick me up and bring me back home, but only after the windshield on the truck was replaced and only after taking me back to the psychiatric ward. I did not want to go. Against the advice from the doctor there, they released me into my folks' care. The psychiatrist (all of them) diagnosed me as having the neurological malfunction of being Bi-Polar. (I prefer Manic Depressive, as it is so much more punk rock). This "disorder" I think was a misdiagnosis and a sloppy one at that. The problem of "mania" has not yet occurred since and it has almost been sixteen years. The only time in my life in which this has happened was after taking those Satan pills. The whole of the situation was my fault though, after all. Who is guiltiest? The one taking the poison or the one dispensing the poison? I do not have Bi-Polar Syndrome. And THAT is my story.

Manic Me.

Manic me, me manic.

Here I am, to take over the Earth.

Here I am, to take over the sea. Here I am.

Me manic. Manic me.

To gain my prize at any cost.

To curse and bleed those loved.

To let nothing in my grasp go free.

Here I let all thing inside die: Not be.

Here I go. Manic me.

(Poem written while under that evil spell.)

Crush

The computer sounded over the PA: "*Inmates, this facility has a horizontal crush level of 10% today for all cells.*" "*Inmate 801, it is now your meal time. You have fifteen minutes to be back in your cell.*"

My cell door opened and my rear wall moved to the front of my cage prompting me into a tunnel with a brightly lit room at the end of it. There was a park-bench styled table that was made of concrete and resided in the middle of this small sphere-shaped room. Atop the middle of the table sat my one meal for the day. Pink hot mush with a cup of milk and a plastic glass of water. This stuff tasted like coppery, gritty mashed potatoes with a non-descript meat blended in it: this meal is what I had yesterday, this meal is what I'll have tomorrow, and this meal is every day's ration. So being back to my holding area usually was not a problem. If I was not back inside cell five in pod four on time, gas would fill the feeding area and that stuff is nasty! The computer says that there are no long term physical effects on humans though. I do not think the computer has lied as of yet. The gas is like breathing fire in and out all day and it seems to last for days, as if Hell resided nowhere else other than in your chest. This place offers many things like that, including solitude.

I got up this morning not knowing where I was. I say morning tentatively; morning is whenever you wake up. Evening is whenever you fall asleep. Lighting in this room is always the same and one sleeps here naked on a concrete floor. The temperature is warm but not uncomfortably so. My cage, at times, is perfectly square because of the facility's Crush Level, in this moment however it is rectangular. The floor cement is perfectly flat but has a small hole for human refuse in it; also built in are deep but thin slots that are designed for drainage. Sometimes the Crush Level can be at 80% or even 90%; it really can be whatever the computer deems appropriate for any particular day or time, and of course it can be as bad as having a 100% Crush Level. Cells can also have different Crush Levels for individual offenders depending on their crime on the outside or their behavior on the inside. The entrance, or front wall, of my place is made of some kind of indestructible, clear, hybrid Plexiglass that can also double as a computer screen. Most of the time the screen just looks like a cement wall, but at random times the computer broadcasts "important" messages to help inmates when they are released from this correctional facility. The computer will say things like: *"Be good to your Care Takers, for they are good to you"* and *"Just as the head must control one's hands, the Care Takers must control the Cared For; both must act as one"* and *"Remember, obedience is freedom and freedom can be taken away."*

Life on the outside is better than being on the inside of Correctional Facility #1; this is a general, but not congenial, feeling held in the hearts of the Cared For. Though the sun still shines, the birds still sing, and the sky is still blue, there is always this sense of perfect cleanliness, perfect sterility, and a perfect burden. The outside world has an orderliness that seems chaotic, like humanity cares for nothing more than to keep themselves in a cogged clock-like existence. Humankind, though natural, seems like an actual affront to nature and it is the Care Takers that have the onus of enforcing this vile joke.

The cities that have been built by the Cared For have been designed by the Care Takers and are many on our small planet. Each city stands like an island devoted to sterility, surrounded by the chaos and jungles of nature's lawlessness. Our cities are devoted to the insanity of total law and law enforcement. Rules and regulations stacked upon more rules and regulation. We do not use paper anymore, but if we did, our society and our planet would be nothing more than a big ball of spinning white space trash made from the burdens we have placed upon our own shoulders. Rules are always enforced too, rules and orders handed down by the trillions, rules that clash with one another in a trillion separate ways. Even if one tries to follow the laws and abide by this madness they would do so to one's own detriment; he or she would always be guilty, always be guilty of something.

"It is so decreed by your Care Takers that the Cared For be shielded and protected from themselves, for they

have been born in sin; they have ALL been born guilty! Law, and following that law, is now humanity's only grace."

Living life this way is, of course, a travesty and a complete distortion of what a just and right world should be like. Living under such rule is a complete mess! On the outside of Facility #1, you can still step across the threshold of one's residence and onto one's front yard and stretch your arms and legs out below a beautiful sky and breath in the freshest of air, but only at certain times. There is no Crush Level though. That is nice. In order to find freedom in these city-states that we now live in, the Care Takers give free advice to the Cared For like, *"Through hard work YOU can work away your sin"* and *"Through sweat and sweet work you, too, can become a Care Taker, blameless and right."* Inspiration at its best! I have yet to see a Cared For become a Care Taker (actually I have yet to see a Care Taker), but it would be the dream if there were any dreams around here.

The cities have been built with fortified walls that have no openings, in order to keep the chaos of nature out, that tangled, garbled assortment of horribly unfettered life. These walls also keep the lovely and fettered humans within the circles of the cities. The air in these micro-polis clusters is pristine as they are surrounded by thick forest and jungles of green, and the only kind of traffic we have is foot traffic. The next circular layer of these city onions are made of tenements that also complete a lesser circle and house the populations of each city. These apartments are separated by thin paths that lead to the heart of a city. In the next layer we find gardens and farming patches also divided by pathways. In the middle of each city isle lies The Work Place and next to each Work Place is a Facility #1.

My job in The Work Place every single day, is this: I run on a treadmill for one hour and then I go and row on a row machine for one hour and so on and so forth. I do this with thousands of other work mates for eight hours a day. What we get out of the treadmills and row machines is electricity, so that we can power the Computer, Facility #1, and the rest of our city. There are lots of neat gadgets around here that need electric power, like the giant knife blades that slide around the top of the city ramparts at lightning speed in order to keep the *Chaos of Nature* out, and our magnetic catapults that jettison refuse outside the city walls to blacken Nature's eyes.

"Today's Crush Level is 50%," the Computer stated. How I became inmate 801 in Facility #1 is this: I hate treadmills and row machines! I have been what our society calls an Electrician for years and it just gets tiresome, physically, emotionally, and, worst of all, egotistically! I had a dream last "night" that the walls of Facility #1 opened up and The Computer had said that I was free to go. I started to jog, and then run, finally I was sprinting with all of my might, but I was getting nowhere and then I stopped and looked down and saw that I was on a treadmill. I woke up and tried to stand but I smashed the side of my head into concrete and bled a little. The Computer told me this morning that *"A body is a terrible*

thing to waste." Did The Computer know my thoughts? My dreams?

After that my front wall started showing a mountain meadow with tall grass and flowers waving in the wind, with a backdrop of glaciered peaks surrounded by deep blue sky. Birds were chirping happily, the wind was whispering softly, and beyond these sounds seemed to resound a peaceful silence. At the same time my ceiling started to lower from 50% to more and more of a crush level. It kept on lowering until I was splayed out flat with both of my wrists at my side in a gingerbread man position. My head was forced sideways but facing the screen. Now, I only saw the grass and flowers waving at me as the birds became extremely loud and the gentle breeze sounded with the fury of a tornado. My chest was pinned to the floor and it seemed that with each breath out, I would inhale less air; to move air became almost impossible. The Computer told me *"Stay calm 801. Be calm."* Then, even louder than the breeze and gay birds, The Computer commanded, *"A body is a terrible thing to waste, 801. Minds do not matter, 801. A body is a terrible thing to waste, 801. Minds do not matter, 801."* This went on until my "day" ended and I was finally calm enough to pass out.

On the outside the people say that Facility #1 has a 70% successful rehabilitation rate, but that figure goes to 5% if you are a second-time offender. I remember one peaceful evening after being done with a shift at The Work Place: I had just finished my dinner and I was washing dishes when all of my walls and my ceiling turned into broadcasting screens. The image was of a second-time offender, an eight-year-old boy who was pinned against a concrete floor, splayed out like a ginger child. The filming devices focused in on his terrified, bulging eyes and his pressurized head. The Computer reminded all: *"Now children, remember to always obey your mother and your father. Because mother and father obey as well."* I knew what was to come. All of my neighbors knew what was to come. We all went out of our apartments and into our front yards standing out there in the freshest of air, watching an amazing sunset with colors I am too inept to even describe. We all stood there and marveled at that setting magic: silently.

If being a Cared For on the inside or outside seems like torture then you would be right. However, there is no Crush Level on the outside and we get to eat vegetables and good meat. The Cared For always wonder what it is that the Care Takers eat or where they live, as they do not live with us. Who are they? Do they even exist? Are they gods? Do they reside on some sort of newfangled Mount Olympus? Can we really become one of them? Did they program The Computer? Is The Computer the Care Takers? Is The Computer god? What the fuck is that pink mush? One at this level and, thus confined in and out of Facility #1, can only guess, but I have never seen a Care Taker and that bothers me. That one question keeps coming to my mind: Do the Care Takers even exist?

We, the people of this particular polis, have heard legends of bands of malnourished, senile, ancient people roaming through the jungles beyond our walls, starving to death and eating one another, but only after one had perished from starvation. *"On the outside of these godly city walls lie only privation, hunger, and death. Blessed are those within this city's embrace."* Was it a Care Taker that said that or The Computer?

There are also murmurs and mumblings of ghostly voices out there in the jungles at night. These voices speak of youth, strength, and lives being lost slaving for one great savage machine. A machine that connects over the entirety of this planet. These woeful phantom voices come on the darkest of eves, when we are dragooned out of our tenements and into our yards by the violence on our home walls. It is against the law to speak of these legends. It is against the law to think of these voices. It is against the law to wonder about the souls from which these ephemeral chants spring. It is against the law to dream of them!

"Your name, 801, is Tanner Gooding. Did you hear me, 801? Your name is Tanner Gooding. DID YOU HEAR ME, 801! I SAID YOUR NAME IS TANNER GOODING!" I screamed back "ALL RIGHT, FUCK! MY NAME IS TANNER GOODING!" I was seated in a group of elderly people that formed a circle around a fire. All seemed worn, but healthy for their age. All gave off a sense of warmth on the inside, as if not just warmed by the fire. I could feel their warmth. I could feel them on the inside, viscerally. I felt their love for me. Around that burning, hypnotic fire, I stared as those around me disappeared one by one: then there was only darkness and fire. The voices of these beings were still with me and they began to tell me a story.

"Tanner, you have always been Tanner Gooding. We all have names; we no longer have numbers. We are not a part of some silly device that files our souls and ear tags each one in cataloged order to be used and used until our bodies can spend no more for The Computer. That god! We are beings of light; each one of us, though, possess a fleshy body, Tanner. We cannot be killed by that electrical appliance with artificial intelligence programmed by beings of flesh years ago. You have started to question everyday life in the city, Tanner, and that is now why you can hear us. You will not be rehabilitated. Tanner, we are the Care Takers, we had our bodies worked until later in life, and then we were catapulted out of the city and into a large and deep lake. Most of the Cared For do not make it and that's why swimming is illegal in your particular city. Others impact the water so hard they sustain injuries which we cannot mend; those suffer greatly because of this—they are mercy killed. The sayings that you've heard, reportedly from the Care Takers, of course, were fraudulent. You have always known this. On the darkest of nights we offer prayers to those that are willing to open their hearts to other possibilities outside The Computer's laws. You have opened your heart, Tanner. One day, you too can live with us in peace and happiness. However, when you awake, your cell will be at a 100% Crush Level.

You will be born again, Tanner! Remember though, through your spirit, I hope this message remains!" Then...

"WE INTERUPT THIS DREAM FOR A VERY IMPORTANT BROADCAST! *"Work Tanner! Work! Work! Work! For your god The COMPUTER! Eat that pink sludge, 801: eat the bodies of your fellow electricians, Tanner. Do not let them die in vain! Slurp! Slurp down your fellow Cared For so that you can be rehabilitated. If I crush you when you wake, the Care Takers are right, 801, you will be born again. Born to slave for me. WORK! WORK! WORK! FOR ME! If I crush you, Tanner, your body will sustain those that can be rehabilitated and they will power me. You will always be my slave, in life and in death. Sing along, 801. Sing along, Mr. Gooding! Sing along, Tanner! La,la,la,la,la...CRUSH! CRUSH! CRUSH! CRUSH! CRUSH! HA! HA! HA! HA! HA! DIE! DIE! DIE! DIE! DIE!"*

*** *

Jesus! My heart won't stop pounding. I can't catch my breath! I'm going to have a heart attack. Stay calm, Tanner. Control yourself! Tanner? Fuck! Calm, be calm. Your cell is perfectly square; you are going to be okay, 801. My name is 801 isn't it? I want to be rehabilitated. I don't want to die! Be calm. Okay, everything is okay. Rehabilitation is all I want. I want to be back on the treadmill. I want to be an electrician!

"You hear me Computer? I WANT TO BE AN ELECTRICIAN! I want to be rehabilitated!" Born again into this? To live this life over? The only way out is to be rehabilitated and work until I'm old and used up. Oh, I want outside the city's walls! Used up is the only way out or this cycle will never end! "Computer do you hear me? I WANT TO BE REHABILITATED! I HAVE SINNED! I'M YOURS COMPUTER. DO WITH ME AS YOU WILL!" -Now the screen sounds- *"Relax 801, I hear you. Be calm, Mr. Gooding. You will have peace. Stay calm. Be at peace. Be at peace, for today your cell's Crush Level is scheduled to be 100%. Have a nice day."*

Wrecks

I was driving over a high pass. There was snow on the road, a large rock in front of me, and then a sick, slow sliding of my car over the side into darkness. There was nothing I could do! I felt a sudden acceleration laterally, vertically, horizontally, over and over: I was spinning; everything was black. My stomach churned and dropped nauseously and this feeling seemed to last forever: churning and spinning in the dark, churning and spinning and fearing in my fall, churning and spinning falling through the dark.

Silence. Cold. There was nothing but silence and cold when I awoke. I could not feel my feet. I could not feel my hands. My limbs were frozen. The car had landed upright; the snow was landing on my face. All of the windows had been busted out and there was blood all over the place! It was cold. I was shivering. I was scared. This was the first winter storm of the season. I left the apartment with flip flops on. I was in the wilderness. I could not move. I was alone. *Stupid! Stupid! Stupid!* The engine would not turn. I only had a T-shirt on that was frozen in blood. My teeth were chipping from shivering. I could not stop shivering! I was alone at the bottom of a deep canyon. Out of sight. I was in the wilderness. I was nauseated and scared. I prayed to Jehovah. So alone! So cold! Then everything disappeared.

When I awoke a second time, I was warm and so was the blood around me. I could not see my legs or lap. I had a tremendous pressure in my head. The dash had folded me into the tangled structure of my automobile and I felt like I was being eaten by my car. I could move my arms now, but my lower half, just above my navel, was enveloped. It was like being the head of a toothpaste tube with bottom rolled up so one could get every bit of paste out. Ahhh! The pressure in my head made my ears ring and my mind echo with a high pitch hum! I could hear traffic all around me and honking horns accompanied with screeching tires. A warm drizzle was wetting my face because the firefighters had removed the roof of my tacoed coffin. I was terror-stricken and taking deep gasps of air through an oxygen mask. The mask was not helping. I heard a man say, "Poor bastard. When we move the car, this fuck is going to bleed out before we can get the shock pants on. Anyone find a family contact?" Then someone answered "Hey stupid shits. We don't have time for that. Chief wants this car out of here NOW! We need to get traffic moving! Jesus. You pussies act like this is your first wreck!" I couldn't control how sad I felt and I couldn't stop crying. All I wanted was my mother!

Blank, then zap! I was back driving down another road, scared shitless with a feeling of pure dread. I couldn't slow the car down. I was traveling the speed limit of sixty miles an hour, but I couldn't go anywhere other than down this one country road. I was not in control of the only vehicle traveling west. The car, however, stayed on track like it was on a pair of invisible rails. I couldn't unlock the doors or get the windows to open. I broke my fist against the windows; they seemed to be made of granite. I could not get the seat belt to unfasten as I painfully smashed my broken fingers into its button. I was no longer sad, but again terror filled. The radio was playing an endless song that kept on getting louder and louder and faster and faster as it was keeping time with my panicked heart.

In the opposing lane, traveling east, millions of trucks, cars, vans, tractor-trailer combos, RVs, motorcyclists, and cyclists were zooming by in a never-ending procession as far as my eyes could see, all of them seeming to speed and go faster with each passing moment. They swerved wildly as I went by and they sounded like race cars going by a stationary microphone while one was watching NASCAR. All the while, deer, elk, bears, mountain lions, and every sort of forest animal, wanted a suicide's death by crossing this rural thoroughfare. The tractor-trailers were passing the bicyclist, the cars were passing the tractor-trailers, and the motorcycles were passing the cars. Each vehicle passing was offering me a new chance at death.

I was a sweating mess! My heart was racing as fast as the cars. Faster and faster, the mad motorists came at me as my heart pumped louder and louder. DEATH, DEATH and more death came, too, as the creatures crossing kept dying faster and faster, like a psychotic, living and breathing version of Frogger. A pink misty cloud started to appear over this insane highway as animals were getting hit by the thousands. My car started to hydroplane as the highway filled with blood. My windshield wipers came on automatically, as did the windshield sprayers. Faster and faster, they wiped and rinsed away the life blood of the forest creatures. My car was bathing in blood! I was still able to see the horrors stretched out before my eyes though, and before me the line of death quickened its already lightning pace, as they now formed a single blurry solid line of pitched fury. I feared more and more. My heart pounded harder, faster, louder! Until...RING! RING! RING!

"Dude! I woke up soaked in sweat with my heart beating crazy fast! I didn't feel like I slept at all last night and I was going to be late for work this morning. I didn't even have time to shave, shit, or shower! However, me being the guy I am, I still had the fortitude to get in my car and drive west to work. Even with that sick feeling in my gut. Because, that's the kind of employee I am, boss! Faithfull! I am your guy chief! A total and complete yes man. You shouldn't even worry about the fifteen minutes I was late. I've only been late five times this month!"

Mozart

Sometimes I would get paranoid. I used to think to myself, "Well now, I could be one of the greats." You see, at one time I played a guitar just like Johnny B. I played many instruments like Mr. Good. All of my life, before the accident, I was told that I was of great musical talent and that if I kept it up, "You'll go places with it one day, Mozart." All of my friends and family paid me lip service in that way. Once in a while I believed it was true; most of the time, though, I wondered if it was. I knew that they were just being nice and they did not want to hurt me. However, when stressed, they'd also tell the truth.

You see, I had been "good" for a very long time. You can even watch clips of me on TV as a child prodigy playing the violin. I was destined for a height of heights. I was the natural. Later, as a young man, I started doing my own compositions and I had mastered over sixteen instruments. I loved making my own music! I used to work on it for twenty hours a day and not even notice the sun come up or go down or my folks going in or out of the house. One day, fifty years ago, my father came into my room early in the morning after I had stayed up all night finishing one of my best pieces yet. He grabbed my pillow from under my head and started hitting me with it, then slapped me awake with his hands screaming, "Get up you lazy piece of shit! Get up and get some work! What you do here is not work! WE ALL HAVE TO WORK! YOU ARE NOT

SPECIAL! YOU'RE GOING OUT RIGHT NOW MOZART, YOU BASTARD!" He then got my dress clothes from my closet (including my tie and dress shoes) and put me in a headlock, dragged me out of my room, and pushed me out the front door of the house in my underwear. I landed on the concrete walkway in a supine position. He yelled, "HAPPY JOB HUNT YOU SPECIAL SON OF A BITCH!" Then he slammed the door behind him.

When I'm paranoid, I wonder if there are others in my way, or, if by some human construct, some have already been chosen for greatness while others have been predetermined to be workers. And it does not matter what work they do, just so long as they produced. I think now, that it did not matter how much time and effort I put into that old love of mine; I would never have been seen as able to reach full human potential, and now, as an adult, everything I did as a child has been forgotten. It seems that there are so many of us humans that we all get lost in the muck. With each child born, our own value slips down the human worth meter, or in some third world country, another child must die if one is born here. Like I said though, I can be paranoid.

Fifty years ago today, that is when I landed my first and only J.O.B. Life with mom and dad became easier after that. When I was washing other people's dishes, I received their respect. All I had to do was walk three miles to work, clock in, and start scrubbing. My feet got soaked. In the winter here, it got so cold that my shoes froze solid walking home after a shift. The place I worked at didn't provide waterproof aprons (and still does not), so I made my own using trashcan liners. In back of the kitchen, I'd be alone and the only people I'd speak to were the other dishwashers. This made it easy not to reproduce, because when one is a dishwasher the waitresses, and all girls, leave you alone. In the pit, dirty plates came back by the hundreds and I just scrubbed, scrubbed, scrubbed. In my life, I must have cleaned trillions of plates. Is there music in washing dishes? Maybe. Is there blood borne illnesses that the cuts on my hands were exposed to from the bloody gums of some patrons and their slimy silverware? Who knows? Who cares? I just scrub away and have been doing so for fifty years.

You, the reader, might wonder, *"What happened to you, Mozart? What kind of accident did you have?"* Well, my first day as a dishwasher I had not yet procured slip-resistant shoes and I slipped on wet, greasy tile. I hit my head hard on the floor that fortuitous afternoon, and ever since, I have not been able to play or compose music. So I just washed dishes for the rest of my life. Maybe it made me mentally handicapped? Because after my parents died, they left me their house, and I have lived in it the entirety of my life. I live there still. I have no woman. I have little money. I'm a writer. I may be retarded and I get no respect.

Man with Alzheimer's goes on killing spree.

By Bob Page

Associated Press

DURANGO, CO. — Today. A man recently diagnosed with Alzheimer's disease by area physicians was shot to death by local law enforcement, after a drawn out gun battle that lasted eight hours had ended. The man, John R. Memoriesgone, reportedly killed his own son and dog after not recognizing them as beloved members of his household. Also found dead were two cats, one parrot, and one lizard. Neighboring residents said that they heard what they thought to be "automatic gun fire" coming from Mr. Memoriesgone's house and also someone yelling "DON'T TREAD ON ME YOU BASTARDS!"

It is believed his son was killed trying to check on his ailing father after being worried about him not answering phone calls for a period of one week. Sheriff Deputy Phillip Rememberslots said, "It appears that the man mistook his own animals for blood-thirsty, devil-worshipping government agents wanting to take his guns." The man, a prolific collector of guns and other weapons, is also known to have held a credence that one day he would have a stand-off with government officials— that day has come.

The Jerk & The Clerk

Clerk: It's early morning, 2 a.m. The fuckers keep trying to buy beer. Not an option, so they steal it after bartering. Bums come in asking for change and single cigs. Bar patrons pour in and start fights in the store, at the pumps. Police never show up on time. I am here, the guardian of chaos. Last gas for an eastbound traveler heading out across a dark nation. I am always alone on this shit side of town. Waiting. Waiting for something to happen——happen to me.

Jerk: No more beer. No more gas. No more money. Plenty of gun. Plenty of bullets and plenty of bad! I am getting mine tonight! I don't give a fuck! Fuck the police. Fuck my neighbor. Fuck society. Fuck the Golden Rule. Fuck you and fuck me! I am getting mine! All I need for fun is this pack on my back, gun on my side, and the ethics of a demon to free my mind. I don't care about dying. I don't care about jail. I don't care about any lethal injection. All I care about is one night of madness! After a little walk and pep talk. What have we got here? A convenience store? How convenient! A clerk too! This is going to be a blast! That little shit is going to die tonight.

Clerk: It's 3:45 a.m. No one has been in the store now for forty-five minutes. In two hours and fifteen minutes I'll be off for three days; who knows maybe I'll never come back. Sometimes I think, "Do I really need money this bad?" Most of the time I think, "No, no I don't!" It's 3:46 a.m. now and I can see someone out there stirring my way in the dark. He has a backpack on. He's moving purposely toward the store. Great. Another stinking, drunk homeless guy come to make a bargain! I think I will quit. Life is just too short for this kind of shit!

Jerk: Open the door. Step inside. I'm giddy! Take a glance at my victim. Nod. He just stares at me, bored. Stroll back toward the beer. Take me up an eighteener. I stalk from the side. Right hand on my hell sender. Victim stares straight ahead. POP! POP! First one hits. Second one misses. He hits the floor like a squid out of water, just as wet too. "Hey buddy! You might wanna mop up that mess when you get a chance! Someone might, you know...get hurt." Feels good to finally greet him. Go behind the counter, stepping over and through the muck. Get cigs and lotto tickets. Now that my business here is done, it's time to get. "Have a good day buddy!" I like to have an air of professionalism when I pull such gags.

Clerk: The jerk walks in, looks at me and nods. I don't respond. I hope he can feel my disdain. He goes, of course, to the beer section. I wish this place had locks on the beer doors! That way I might not have to argue with him in a second. I can hear him grab a box. I just stare outside, wishing that I was somewhere, anywhere, out there.

FUCK WHAT HAPPENED?!

MY EARS ARE RINGING! MY LEGS DON'T WORK!

THE FLOOR IS NEXT TO MY FACE!

I feel weak...I can't move...I'm going to faint...God please call 911...I think God is calling 911...God is 911. I hear, in a soft voice, through all the ringing, "Hey buddy. You might wanna mop up that mess when you get a chance. Someone might, you know...get hurt." I try to thank him. He sounds like an angel. He must be an angel. The light is white...bright is the light...the light is bright and white...the light...

*****

Jerk: My public defender told me that the prosecutor could recommend a sentence of up to 300 years in prison, or propose some new law that was passed a few days ago called Dumb-a-rubi's Code or some stupid shit like that. He started to explain it to me, but all I heard was blah, blah, blah, dumb shit, dumb shit, dumb shit, blah, blah, blah. I told him, "Look fuck face, I don't give a shit about what they do to me. I'm a BAD MAN! I don't care if they kill me or put me in solitary confinement for months at a time with no TV! In fact, I can't wait to go to prison. It gives me a chance to be bad!" And, to prove I meant it, I shouted to everyone in the courtroom, "THAT'S RIGHT! I'M A BAD MAN! YOU FUCKS! I'M A BAAAAD MOTHERFUCKER! AND I'M GLAD THAT LITTLE BITCH CAN'T WALK, WAVE, OR FUCK ANYMORE! FUCK HIM AND FUCK ALL OF YOU!" After that my public defender put his head on the table and banged it a bit. The judge ordered me gagged and restrained for the remainder of the trial. I kind of liked it. It made me feel like Hannibal Lecter.

Clerk: It has been a year and a half since the night of my last work shift. My last night of doing anything at all really. I'm always strapped into a sitting position in a chair. The places change but my position remains the same. Today I'm in a courtroom. There are a lot of people and media here. I'm on TV. I wish I wasn't here. I'm probably drooling. Earlier my catheter got snagged on something and urine went everywhere. I didn't have a change of clothes. They gave me a blanket. I can still smell. I can't point. Earlier in the trial they wanted me to look in the direction of the man that did this to me. I can still see. I saw him. I can still fear. I can't move my arms or my legs. I don't know what I feel. I don't want to be here right now.

The prosecutor said they needed my permission to seek a new form of punishment called Hammurabi's Code. It's a new option for victims and judges to equal out what people call "real justice." The code came from an old Babylonian king. The code was quietly passed into law just a few days ago. It's known to have started the saying "an eye for an eye and a tooth for a tooth." I asked my attorney, "Now what does that exactly mean to me?" He said, "I don't know exactly what the judge will recommend. But, after he has a talk with you he could conclude that the state should surgically inflict upon the defendant the same injury you sustained after being shot. Basically, they will make sure he becomes, and I don't mean to be disrespectful here, a quadriplegic too. I have to warn you though, he will not do any jail time other than what he has already served." I started to feel something. I started to feel something warm inside. I started to feel good, I think giddy even. I think I feel justice!

Jerk: The jury's verdict on all the counts was guilty. I am sitting before the judge waiting to be sentenced. I am still gagged and restrained. I know I'm going away for the rest of my life. Three hots and a cot for the rest of my life! It's almost too good to be true! I can't wait to hear it from the judge!

Clerk: My attacker sits on the other side of the courtroom from me. Gagged and strapped into a restraining chair. I kind of like that, but I get the feeling that he does also. The judge is explaining Hammurabi's Code to everyone and that this is the first instance in modern time that it will be enforced. My assailant is starting to look uncomfortable. In fact, he's looking down right restless; he's wiggling like a worm. I guess the "bad man" doesn't like his chair anymore! The gavel has landed. The words "so be it" have been said. The strapped in jerk is actually making the chair come off the floor! He is mumbling something super loud! I cannot make it out while that ball is in his mouth! His eyes are bursting out of his head! Oh! Whoopsie! The "bad man" just made the chair flip, smashing his face. It looks like he may have broken his nose. I haven't been this entertained since my dad took me to the circus when I was five. This isn't just entertainment. This is justice!

Jerk: Surgically sever my spine near C4? Hammurabi? An eye for a tooth and a tooth for an eye? What does this mean? Turned back out onto the streets? What?

"The citizens of this great state will not squander one more penny of taxed subsidies on you for any medical, food, or shelter cost, nor will they provide you with a wheeled chair. Mr. Chandler, you are to be cast out onto the streets a quadriplegic! To become what you have yourself done to your fellow man! Cast into a city that has a climate almost as cold as your own heart. Mr. Chandler, right now surgeons await you in the next room. They are ready for you now. Beyond those surgery walls are the streets Mr. Chandler. You will be put there for all to see. For all to see what real justice is. There, on that cold hard cement, with your head on the ground, lying in your own incontinence you will stay. You will either lie there until you perish or your fellow man takes mercy on your soul...May your fellow man take mercy on your soul! So be it. Mr. Chandler, the state has spoken!"

Ahhh! What does this all mean? A quadriplegic? I've got this fucking ball in my mouth! Let me out of this chair! They won't let me speak!? "IHMHMHMFFFFFFFFFF! UMMMHMMMFFFFFFFF! IMMUGHUFFFFFFFF!FFFFF!EEEEEEMMMMMM!" Goddammit, they must let me talk! I wasn't ready for this! They can't do this! I'm a human being! This is wrong! This is too soon! This is not justice! I want my justice! They didn't inform me! God help me please! I don't deserve this! God save me! I don't deserve this! No God! No! "IMMHMMMMUMMMHHUMMMUMMMUMMMMM! NOOOOO! IMMMHUUMMMMAHHHHMMMMMMMAAAHHHHHMM MMMMMMM!"

The Block

The sign on the wall next to the time clock read, "One's capacity for success is only limited by one's capacity for hard work," or something similarly enlightening. I thought about this motivational sign as I rode my bicycle six miles home into a forty-mile-an-hour headwind at 10 p.m. after working a slight five-hour shift in Shitsville. It didn't seem so hard. But why was I so tired? What is my capacity for hard work? What is my capacity for success?

Tuesday morning started at eight, surprisingly not hungover, but fresh. I got up, made coffee, jumped online, checked the weather for the day, made my habitual net stops, Myspace, Rockclimbing.com, YouTube, went to Google to check out how China, Kosovo, Russia, Iran, U.S., U.K., Pakistan, and the Korean Peninsula were all getting along (they were all talking shit about one another as usual) so they were getting along fine. Took a shower, packed my backpack, put my gym clothes in with my Albertsons costume and other essential bicycle crap, and left the house. It was 11 a.m.

"One's capacity for success is only limited by one's capacity for hard work." I bike six miles to the gym. I lift weights for an hour and a half. I run on the treadmill. I average three seven-minute miles. (I'm trying to get them down to six-minute miles). Once I stop, I go for a quarter-mile swim in a saltwater pool, then shower off and leave the gym. I bike three miles for my DUI class. (I have been court-ordered to take an 18-month alcohol education class for a second DUI. Hence the cycling.) I meet with the counselor for fifteen minutes. She makes sure I've paid. I bike three miles into the wind to work.

I walk into the back of the store where the butcher block is. I pass my manager; she says nothing. I know she is mad. (She's either mad or not mad). I have trouble gauging how mad she is, but I don't worry about it...I'll find that out soon enough. I put on the ridiculous uniform they make us wear. I go to clock in.

The sign next to the time clock says, "One's capacity for success is only limited by one's capacity for hard work." SWIPE...IT'S GO TIME!

Stop! (A short digression of path here.)

If the saying is true, then I must be heading for success...right? However, if you work hard in a place that never rewards you with room for advancement, what does that mean? Does it mean that the hard work is wasted? If your hard work is not a means to an end, and is just a means, then you get nowhere by working hard. It's a treadmill. So tread lightly? I want more than to simply survive. My hard work must go to where my ambitions lay. As in, if I want to survive and survive with any sort of self-respect, spine, balls, or dignity, I must put that hard work into my writing and write to survive, and dump this place, and all places like it.

Go!

I walk back to the block on "Albertsons' time." My manager still says nothing to me. I help a few "valued costumers," all the while listening to her mumble to herself, slamming doors, throwing stuff, and basically being a bitch. Done with serving the entitled people, just for kicks, I ask my manager, "How's it goin'?" From there on it's nothing but one form of verbal abuse after another. She grabs my arm (non-sexual in manner) and proceeds to tow me around so I can see what I did not do yesterday and why I am a horrible person. All the while, she is yapping noisily, cussing and flailing her arms about in a fevered frenzy in front of all the patrons in the meat area. All I hear is YAP, YAP,YAP. (But from the looks on the customers' faces, I can tell it's more than that).

As this is going on I can't help but think. What has happened to this lady? Where does all the pressure she feels come from? Is it really just from me not hand-trimming a few chicken breasts? Am I a bad person? Why doesn't she quit if she hates being here so much? Lady you have a choice...you don't have to do this.

So, I kind of listen to her while she throws her tantrum and clocks out crying. Storming out of the building, never to be seen again until she comes back and guns everybody down, me being the first. (After such a display of crazy, our slogan at work should be "Albertsons: Crazy!" instead of "Albertsons: Crazy About Food"). If I see her in here again tonight, I'm ducking out the back at light speed. A common knee-jerk reaction around here...for me anyway.

R.A.M.M

The next day I go in earlier. This time I have the "pleasure" of wrapping meat for our main meat cutter/boss and resident autistic madman, a.k.a R.A.M.M. When I first get into the cutting room he has to go over how to clean up the bloody room after the cutters have left. R.A.M.M's spew is this, "Bob, I know you're new here, but when I was your age (I'm 30; he's 50) I could wrap for six cutters at once and be ahead of the game. Now, I know you're a good guy and that you are trying...but when you are here I want you to always put your heart and all of your soul's being into this place! Bob, we are a team! We should put everything we've got into making this the best place to buy meat as we can! We are a part of the A-team Bob. THE A-TEAM!" (I know, what does this have to do with cleaning? A little pep prattle there for me).

Let me tell you. This man can talk and talk and talk. About the most routine things and while doing so he wants you to listen intently. While he's talking all you want to do is work and get your shit done so you can go home on time, but R.A.M.M (and his magical ability to talk and be autistic) will stop you while you're working earnestly and say, "Bob…good job on clean up last night…However…do you see these black marks on the freezer door? Tonight can you clean them? Also, can you clean every square inch of the back here (1,600 square feet) with a hand scrubber and sanitizer? Please don't forget to wrap up 300 packages of chicken breast for tomorrow's eight hour sale. I know you only have three hours left of work, but don't go over on the clock. Oh yeah! Can you please keep the case full, face the freezers and restack and put away our new load (10,000 pounds of assorted meat product). Help Jim out with the customers if he's busy tonight; he'll probably be busy. Remember to guide the customers to what else might go good with their purchases. GET THOSE SALES!"

That is just a small part of what retard just said. (I'm not a court reporter and I wasn't taking notes so maybe a quarter of what he told me will get done tonight). By now I have two hours on the clock. He also instructs me that, "Just this time it's okay to work off the clock…just get your stuff done!" He also leaves with this bit: "My goodness, I needed to clock out an hour ago. Really Bob I think you should know this stuff. I'm short on hours I can't just stand here and talk." That is how most days working with R.AM.M. go. I do what I think is a fantastic, beyond dutiful job, only to be told that I suck and, "Your work is mediocre."

Peons.

The other minor actors on the block consist of one eighteen-year-old college kid (who cares just as little about this place as I do and is a pleasure to have around). One homeless man who cares a great deal about his workplace and is more knowledgeable about the meat department and the rest of the store than the store director. He drinks, slurs, serves, steals, drinks, slurs, serves, steals like a repeating rifle. He does not leave the store even when off since he has nowhere to be. (Where do you drop off a homeless date? Yeah, you know). Finally, we have a twenty-three-year-old black father of one and husband to no one. Who does all of the above as well as "hooking the people up" which is his favorite thing (changing tags and the prices of those tags or weight) and while doing so is always shouting, "DID YOU MISS ME?!", "FOE SHOAW!", "KIMBO SLICE!", "WHO GIVES A FUCK?!" and "WHAT-EVA!" These, and only these, senseless sayings he yells...all...day...long.

Then there's me and my sole purpose. Which is to get out of the store on time. Because I've taken this company's slogan, "One's capacity for success is only limited by one's capacity for hard work." And have applied it to my life outside of work. That means I must hurry the fuck up...and hurry I do. My hours are spent in haste doing all of my closing chores at once, filling product, rotating product, selling, anti-selling, manipulating, cleaning floors, the dishes, the drains, making signs, programming the scales (to my liking), sending people to other stores (whose product is FAR superior than our own), lying, practicing first-class customer worshipping, prostrating, quickly debasing myself from one master to the next. I always must get out on time!

From across the counter, it must look like I'm some kind of mythically cartoonish, Tasmanian-devil-like creature spinning around the bloodied block floor. One nice lady asked me if I "had to pee" while my sweat was dripping into her "gourmet" seafood salad. (I'm sure the added salt made it that much more gourmet). "Yes, actually I must pee," I replied, but alas that relief will have to wait for there is another in line! Yee haw! Get those sales! GO! GO! GO!

Mandate 325

I'm going to tell you a story about the not-too-distant now. It's an all-American story. A story about a first world and a third world coming to terms in equality, in humanity and shared grace. A story about the propensity every living soul has for gluttony if given the proper vehicle to deliver it. Let's begin ...

It's 2:43 a.m. and you've been awakened, once again, at a random time of night, by screams from down the hall. Screams that no longer shock you awake, but, while they persist, you can never get back to sleep. The Trimming Squads are harvesting another one of your neighbor's products ... Fat.

This has been going on ever since our beloved elected leaders passed Mandate 325. Three hundred and twenty five represents the weight no man, woman, or child can surpass without immediate product taking. Strict rules are now in place here in the U.S. of A. After a citizen, regardless of class or race, has exceeded their height weight index for their age group, they will be qualified to have product harvested at any time. Priority for trimming takes place as an individual gets closer to 325. Micro-scales that transmit data to The Trimming Board have been implanted into the sole of every man, woman, and child to ensure enforcement of Mandate 325.

Looking back, I guess something had to be done. Americans were getting fatter and fatter. They demanded greasy food made FAST! They sat instead of stood. Drove instead of walked. Used elevators instead of stairs. Moving sidewalks instead of sidewalks. Keyboards became obsolete; dictation for writing became standard. Gyms became a thing of the past, and the "Great Outdoors" has mostly been forsaken.

The U.S. economy mirrored its populous: slow and slothful, lethargic, greedy and with no memory of the country's past to move and make. The people were scorned by the rest of the world, by themselves even. Measures by government to get the whole of the country back to its old glory failed. Dietary laws were established, but met with revolt. A thriving black market of fast food quickly came into place. Crime, gangsterism, and lawlessness by most of the U.S citizenry threatened to send the country into an anarchy of heavy indolence and selfishness. Since the people of this once wonderful nation no longer had a will for greatness, "greatness" would be forced upon them. Mandate 325 was born.

Now while all of this was taking place the rest of the world was going hungry. There seemed to be less and less food to go around. There were no longer Second World countries just one First World and the rest Third World. The bloated glut of the fifty United States was being felt in the bellies of the rest of humanity. Reasons for war with the "rest" to feed the "best" started somewhat benignly.

Propaganda against socialism, communism, terrorism, then went on to things a little more honest like fighting for control of oil, fighting for your right to take. Take whatever. The status quo that Americans as a whole had the rights to everything produced by the rest of mankind. The hard, back-breaking work that was once done for oneself for pride and gain of oneself. Became the back-breaking work of foreign strangers to support the great weight of one heavy nation. Most of mankind was being flogged into the ground...something had to give. And so it was, Americans had to give back.

After bloodshed and rebellion set in worldwide, minus one nation. The leaders of the number one country came to a conclusion that something had to be given as a concession to the hungry emaciated people of the world and at least for the time being, end the revolts. It came to be that the US would give to the rest of the world, and its product would be fat!

Mandate 325 arrived in the form of flash-frozen packages of human flesh, airlifted and dropped from the skies all around this blue planet. No package weighed over 325 pounds. Starving children all over the globe rejoiced! No longer would the kids have to go to work with the pangs of hunger deep inside! A renewed sense of oneness with ALL humans fell upon humanity! The revolts ended. The mandate was a complete success. Mines and clothing sweatshops started to produce again and pump with a renewed vim and vigor! Peace and security fell upon the land due to one simple law.

Here our story ends with a final and compelling thought. That we as the people on this round orb hurling through space and time are connected in one way or another for good or bad, like it or not. In one big cycle of karmic justice. Let's think about the people in this last story of gluttony, along with the proper means to deliver it fairly to everyone and to share and share alike. Be good to one another before goodness is forced upon you. Remember Mandate 325.

A Hearty Lunch

It was my second day working as an EMT in Bakersfield, California, for Gall Ambulance Service. I had just received my certificate as a bona fide, lifesaving hero. I was armed with extensive knowledge and superior medical training: one semester of basic anatomy, physiology, one G.E.D (to get into the program I needed a good enough diploma) and a few months to learn the automatic responses to any given emergency situation...we called this memorized reflex, protocol. Like I said, superior training. I was ready for anything!

It was a Friday around lunch hour. We received a call for a "priority one" man down at a Denny's on Buck Owens's Dr. cross of Rosedale Hwy. We responded with lights and sirens. We got to the parking lot and were greeted by the manager immediately. He repeatedly said that the man was unconscious, but was still breathing and had a strong pulse. The man we found was on his back in front of the hosting area, blue and grayish in tone. Apparently his body signs did NOT completely align with the altruistic manager's story. (I say this in a slightly sarcastic way because I can see where our host is coming from. He doesn't want to do CPR. Would you want to press your lips against the mouth of some old, strange dude who just hit a home run with his Grand Slam breakfast, pitched with a strawberry shake and coffee? Americans eat for this kind of end! All the while, your knees are stewing in his urine and shit because this dead man has lost ALL normal muscle function. Let me answer this question for you...no you would not! You would calm those patrons down. Tell 'em it's all okay and that professional help is on the way...that professional help would be me...Bob and company.)

When the "heroes" came in, we had everything we needed to take care of this sort of mess. We found the patient in a supine position, not breathing; his airway was blocked fully with vomit; he had no pulse. The patient was incontinent and a deep bluish-purple color. As an EMT, I threw in a tongue depressor, pulled out a BVM, and connected it to the oxygen tank then started bagging and doing CPR with a firefighter. My paramedic partner started doing his stuff, prepping to intubate. Once the dead guy was tubed, he administered epinephrine and atropine, but none of this did any good: the monitor still showed asystole (flatline).

The manager told our audience that all was well and to continue eating their sludge. "The patient has a strong pulse and is breathing...he's going with the ambulance crew to the ER for three hots and a cot." And that was that...we were off.

After having left my EMT position, I've been told I should go back into the medical field. I already know it's not for me. I always felt so inept and "Gump-a-fied" when I'd arrive to these situations, situations for which I felt inadequately trained. I always thought, Man you don't need me or my partner; what you and your fucked-up-self need is a doctor! This was the first time (of many) I've performed CPR. Most of the times the results were less than satisfactory. This particular call, my focus was side-tracked. (I kinda had stage fright as we were working this guy up in front of an audience of sixty. This was my first cardiac arrest). I went into some weird mental haze where I could automatically do what was required of me, but I also focused on the uninterrupted clinging and clanging of forks against plates. The bullshitting and laughter of the diners going on as if nothing out of the ordinary was taking place. It almost had the atmosphere of a dinner at Medieval Times.

Later I thought to myself, "So this is how one most likely ends. Not in a blazing fireball of excitement and rarity. But in a Denny's restaurant at the age of seventy five with your own piss and shit all over your corpse. In front of a bunch of laughing strangers that could not care any less and a loving quietly hysterical wife that thought the world of you. That is how most of us will end. Except we probably won't have anyone that loves us. That is ironic."

Bury Me.

Bury me! That is what I want. Bury me with no barrier between my body and the earth and worms. Bury me with no barrier between the roots and the green that has sprung. Bury me very deep, until I am absolutely forgotten. Bury me until everything is new.   ~Bob Page~

LOTTO

01, 33, 41, 16, 55, 07: those were the numbers that changed Jim's life. Jim was a normal man. A powerless man who had always dreamed of power. Those were the numbers on his ticket ... that ticket was a lotto ticket.

You see, Jim was a rather poor fellow. At this point in his life he was living in his small 20-year-old pickup. This beat hunk had a shell that contained everything he needed for day-to-day living. In it lay a futon, a camping stove, a sleeping bag, canned goods, bottled water and canned beer, a few wack-off mags and one copy of The Prince by Niccolo Machiavelli. Jim was not homeless. The truck was his home. He was, however, jobless, but with an income. His income amounted to $800 dollars a month that came to his PO Box from the disability gods. Some doc had said he was nuts (bipolar was the term he used). Jim had insisted that he was just on drugs. However, once the doc told him about a disability stipend from the great state of California Jim insisted he was bipolar! Eight hundred dollars. FREE! Plenty enough for life on the cheap...and to Jim...life was cheap.

Years of working as a low-paid asshole had taught Jim that his life was cheap. His life, as viewed by others, was worth nary a dime. Oh boy, did the shit jobs he's done throughout his life reinforce this notion! Over and over again, he toiled and plodded through some of the most mind-numbing, mind-dumbing, mind-INSULTING jobs on

God's shit-filled earth...and because of this, Jim's lesson was learned. That life, his and others, was cheap.

In Jim's mind he was a BIG man. Why did a big man have to take orders? Why did a big man have to be polite? Humble? Furthermore, why did HE have to be polite, humble and groveling to lesser beings? And they were always lesser beings! The lesser, the more orders on how to do things supposedly better. The lesser, the more constantly annoying and on his back. Lesser beings. Individuals (or robots rather) with the IQ of 70, 80, 90, but never seemingly more than 100. Retards with authority. They always take managerial positions. When they should just fuck off...and leave poor ol' Jim alone.

Jim was feeling nice and alone when he pulled up to the gas station one fine afternoon. It was blazing hot that day, with dry, superheated air capriciously buffeting everything with sand and up-rooted tumble weeds. The sand went everywhere too! Up ones nose, into the mouth, ears, eyes and all nether holes! That was the normal, high-desert weather that suited Jim's sand-pitted truck and face very well. Good weather for a day of winning. Weather like that makes one fancy the idea of lotto-ticket purchasing on a whim. On a whim maybe he could change the weather. Whim being maybe his life. Whim being maybe change the value others placed on him. Whim being maybe he could become a hum-whim-being. So Jim bought one ticket.

Jim let the machine pick out the numbers for him. You know, really leave it up to fate this time he thought. He always despised those bastards in front of him in line that took forever dealing with lotto gambling at a gas station, when he usually bet on the sure things of gas, beer, smokes, and Gatorade. He always seemed to be in a big rush to get to the beer and the desert on the edge of town where he always parked to drink and scream obscenities at the moon: "THIS IS MY EARTH AND UNIVERSE and I! AM! The one being benevolent and piteous enough to others whom I let share MY world. IT WAS NOT GOD! MOTHER FUCKERS! BUT ME!" And yada, yada, yada until the wee hours of the morning when he passed out. Yup, our boy Jim was always in a hurry. In fact it seemed every line he'd ever been queued up in put him in a instant hurry. A silent frenzy within to finish.

01, 33, 41, 16, 55, 07 the newspaper read. Jim looked at his ticket. Jim looked again at the paper. Then finally he put the ticket right up to the numbers in the paper. He repeated this for the next ten minutes. He did win. Now what? He had to call in immediately to claim that at least he thought he had won. A prize that by itself would be the biggest in lotto history. It had gone on with no winners for nearly a year. The sum of which was nearly one billion dollars: $956 million in fact.

Once one has won the lottery, a lot of questions surface. A lot of them greedy and selfish, which Jim did not deny being...he was. After all, Jim thought, "It is in man's nature to be selfish. It's a survival trait and a good one. If one does anything, no matter how small, it's almost always to benefit that one person. Whether it be a smile or simple greeting of 'hello.' These small acts meant that a person wanted whomever to think of them for the time being as, at the very least, a pleasant person. A self-gratifying act indeed. Greed was just a simple matter of degree and perspective. Big or small, it was all the same. Human nature."

So the questions came. How much would ol' Jim get? Would ol' Jimbo have to share? How many would Jim have to share with? How much taxes would the bastards take? How much was ol' Jim's take? How much could he take in one lump sum? How many vultures would come after him with "business partnerships"? Would the vultures have anything to offer other than fund deletion? What did Jim want? A house? A car? A business of some kind? A harem of one hundred, thirty-five-year-old virgins? (At least they'd be fifteen years younger.) Did he want new looks? A larger phallus? To be charitable? Or did he want unbridled, unequivocal power? "Hmmmm," Jim thought. That last question made him smile. Made him feel all warm and fuzzy. Made his spirit rise with ebullient gusto. "YES! POWER! EUREKA!" He had found it.

Power. That was what Jim bought with his lotto money. It was a lucky turn to win. He also came up lucky in another area. He didn't have to share his luck. There were no other winners. Taxes did take a large portion. Also, Jim decided that what he wanted to buy required him to take his money in one lump sum. That too would lessen the fun. Once it was all done, pictures taken, interviews interviewed, pats on the back patted, Jim walked away with a measly 495 million dollars—measly in his miserly mind anyway. Oh, yes there is always something to complain about!

The power Jim bought came in the form of one old, cold, war-relic nuclear bomb. A slimmed-downed and lighter-weight replica, dubbed by the U.S government as the Tsar Bomba, was first detonated by Russia on October 30, 1961. Scientist conjectured it could send a town like Los Angeles to the moon and beyond. It had the potential of blasting miles of Earth with 100 megatons of pure, nuclear rapture, but was reduced to 50 megatons for the test, due to weight concerns. (It still was, however, the largest nuclear weapons test ever performed by mankind, even up to Jim's own time, sixty years later). Jim's bomb was made smaller using the latest alloys and metals, and even plastics, to fit snugly in the back of his small pick-up.

****

December 21, 2021's edition of ABC, CBS and NBC's nightly world news broadcast, all had a new and strangely shocking report. That a fifty-something-year-old man, who had previously won the world's largest lottery five months prior, had acquired a nuclear bomb from a rogue terrorist state in Africa. And the man was now driving around the Los Angeles area with the weapon tied down to the bed of an old, dilapidated truck. And the driver was often drunk. The driver explained incoherently to news reporters and the public that there was some "kind of switch" that he had some surgeon/witch doctor from the jungle put into his chest near his heart "kinda like a heart shocker." In other words, a pacemaker that measured the electrical signals from the heart muscle and if the heart went into a spasm of fibrillation the device would administer a series of shocks to restore the hearts proper rhythm.

"Well" as the man explained while slurring, "the switch was like that. But if my heart stops, then...KABLOOWEEE! TO THE MOON! SMITHEREENS WITH ALL OF YA!"

This last part put a victorious, demon-like smirk on Los Angeles's new captor's face. A face some would admire. Some would loath. But the captor would cherish.

Scientist did in fact confirm Jimbo's story...all of it.

So it came to be, that for a period of six months, Los Angeles and its surrounding area's people were held hostage. By a man whose good fortune had been their bad.

Jim thought this was fantastic!

He went anywhere. Wore anything or nothing. Paid for nothing. Jim was verifiably untouchable! He drank and drove. Sped. Drove with reckless abandon on the 405 backwards, in the wrong direction, for miles at a time. Ate at the finest restaurants. (Those that were still open). Slept in the biggest, most lavished (now abandoned) mansions. Life, now, for Jim. Was good . He now was not just a big man in his own eyes, but also in the eyes of everyone. There was no authority now for him, beyond his own. No laws. No rules. No nothing. No one to tells ol' Jimbo what to do. He didn't drive to the edge of town any longer to yell at the moon while drunk. Now he would drive to the center of the cities he chose and do so. Jim's new and favorite saying to scream in his diatribes to the moon was, "Absolute power corrupts absolutely!" Jim agreed with the old saying. The saying had been marvelously true, of course, and made ol' Jimbo rejoice. But in all of Jim's exaltation, jubilation, and revelry from power mongering, there was one thing he didn't see coming with his power goggles...and that was the end of his reign.

The end that Jim didn't see coming. Came. Through the months of Jim's LA reign, he didn't seem to notice the ever dwindling traffic. In a city filled with millions of cars and folks, he didn't seem to notice the hordes of people leaving what they called the "Future Ground Zero" or LA's "Real Big One" to come. Actually, the city, through the last six months, had become a real ghost town. So much so, that the U.S military was now willing to risk a nuclear explosion in the heart of a now heartless city. After all, Los Angeles was hell on earth anyway. "Why not baptize it in fire," the military generals rationalized.

"We might as will push restart on it...FUCK IT!"

And that was what the world's greatest military minds came up with. They came up with "Fuck it."

They decided they would use a sniper to snipe ol' Jim. One that was young and enjoyed the idea of becoming a legend in martyrism...and so they did.

There was no bang. No boom. No mushroom cloud. No "just deserts" for Los Angeles. No nuclear winter. No doomsday. The crack reported from a lone soldier's rifle and the screeching and crashing of a lone jalopy on a lone freeway....that is all there was... Jim was dead... Jim was duped...The world had been duped. Jim died with no knowledge of being swindled...Jim died a BIG man.

You see, the terrorist state that sold Jim his nuclear dream had a "Nuclear Dream" all of their own. In order to secure funding for their nuclear rights and become a new member of the "Nuclear Club" they sold fakes to reclusive millionaires and billionaires. All for whatever price was right for the social elitist that came their way. After all, with today's prices, it's hard to find a good nuclear bomb under one billion. Rest in peace Jim.

Max Goes for Milk

Witness 1: "Shee-it nigga, that cracker be crazy! He like...I GOTS TO GO! I GOTS TO GO! Motorcycle all screaming, tires be all smokin' 'n' shit! Pfffff, that white boy's gots to get somewheres fast. Ya feel me? Fast! He be like his girl be deliverin' a baby or some shit! But that dude's always like that. AWAYS LIKE THAT!"

Witness 2: "What did I see? Well, at first I heard someone rev-limiting their engine. It sounded like an Indy car. Then I saw white smoke fill up the street and some dude on a rice burner. The guy was doing about forty or fifty in a five-mile-per-hour zone. He didn't even slow down for the speed bump! In fact, I think he was pegging it right over that son of a bitch! Probably got to seventy before the stop sign, which he blew! My family and I just moved into these apartments yesterday. I hope none of our other neighbors are like that! All tweaked out and stupid. This is a pretty shitty place though. The fuckin' guy didn't even have a helmet or shirt on! Jesus man! What have we gotten into?"

Max: *I am fuckin' hungry! All I have in the cupboard is some cereal. What's in the fridge? Nothing. All I want to do is eat some goddamn cereal to start this beautiful day. But no, there is no fucking milk or anything else in this shitty apartment. Nothing is ever simple. It's always fucked. I need a breakfast of champions! I have a bunch of stuff that must be done quickly today. First though, I must get milk! Quick!*

Hop on the bike, push-start it, rev it to 12,000-rpm and GO, GO, GO!

I fly down the alley as fast as the bike will go. Jump the speed bump, run the stop sign, and into the street I ride. I ride through traffic, around traffic, into oncoming traffic, all the while accelerating. I cannot go fast enough. FASTER, FASTER, and FASTER I must move. Green lights, yellow lights, and red, I treat them all the same and with the same speed! Cars, trucks, animals, clip this, clip that, pedestrians and police cars, everyone and everything is an obstacle for me. Nothing will take me from my rhythm. I just react...I am the speed of light!

As I enter the parking lot I hop over a hump, down shift and brake hard. The bike starts to skip and jerk and get squirrely. I hit a cart. It rips one of my mirrors off, then the bike high-sides and I'm catapulted into a bunch of Girl Scouts. (The little ones will now know that the end of life can come at them pretty fast. Also, that cuteness and cookies will not always save them from death or a broken hip. They will learn some of that lesson NOW!) I brush some of them but take out their troop leader. Good thing she weighed more than me, and the bike, because I don't have a helmet on, or a shirt for that matter. She was nice enough not to scream and be all dramatic about it too. After all, she was knocked out, or I simply took her breath away. I can do that to women sometimes. In any, case it was a soft landing, almost comfortable.

Witness 3: "I was ringing up a costumer when I heard a bunch of screaming from the south entrance. There was a motorcycle on the ground between the automatic doors and a bunch of Girl Scouts on the ground. And some dude with no shirt was running full speed to the back of the store. Then, in like a second, he was back again with a quart of milk, running out of the store, throwing all the kids out of the way! He picked up his bike and wheelied out of here. I swear the whole thing only took about thirty seconds!"

Max: *So I "got milk" and now I'm gone. I can taste my breakfast now! Here I come! Taking the same route is out of the question. I think I'm just gonna go straight through the desert, make a quick right and BAM! I peg it! This bike isn't made for this sort of shit and most would say I'm a suicidal ass-hat but I'm a hungry man! Fifty, sixty miles per hour, I jam, no roads, just small brush, dirt and sand, trash and porn. The bike is constantly bottoming and at seventy I am like a motorized skipping stone on the surface of this dusty field. BURN BABY BURN! I might not get to eat breakfast, but I can't stop now! Smash the curb as I enter my apartment complex and both tires blow out. That's okay though, I am sliding into home! Through the garage, bash the door open and throw the bike down on the living room carpet (Warning: That exhaust will burn right through the carpet and padding in a second folks. BE CAREFUL!) and stride right into the kitchen, pour the cereal into the bowl, in goes the milk and there you have it. BREAKFAST!*

The Beer Run

Trapped inside a sea of parked running cars. On some freeway in a large city somewhere. Sits an old boxy beast that spews burned oil fumes and lots of carbon monoxide. The exhaust smells like the rest of the city. In the beast sits a mid-aged balding wreck. Overweight with a big gut that droops over his crotch and rests on his thighs. The man has a thick mustache and hasn't shaved in what appears to be weeks. Dried bits of yellow crust cling to the hairs on his upper lip. While translucent fluid runs from his nose to form more crust. He wears a dirty cotton undershirt that is stained with whiskey, beer and grease from assorted fast food snacks. The man moves his hips from left to right. Smashing his asshole into the seat trying to clear the shit berries that itch and have gathered. They smear and rub off onto the inside of his jeans as he "free-balls" it. The man keeps flailing his arms and shaking his fist at the other parked cars. Yelling and screaming expletives into the smoggy air. Ashes fall from his cigar and burn new holes in his wife beater. Not removing his smoke, he takes a swig of cheap whiskey that's bottled in plastic. Inside, we can hear the man's slurred demands.

"I want a sharp bayonet, lots of ammo, and heaps of meat before my sights goddammit! I am only human, competition is in my blood! Violence is how I get things done. Done for good. I am a beast with wanton fangs! I want to stomp out the anti-ambitious journeys of those around me with big heavy boots. I am an animal...no, better yet...I am a manimal and I serve myself as Job served God! Out of my way! I am my own god! Out of my way! I'm God and I damn you. You wretched little bottom feeders...OUT OF MY WAY!"

He honks his horn again and again.

"Can't those around me recognize my sovereignty? They don't? They don't see it! They don't see my rights. My right of way! They're blind. They're all blind. They must be taught. They must be taught to see. THEY MUST LEARN TO SEE!"

The man honks, revs his engine and drops the clutch, smoking his tires while staying nearly parked.

"They must discern that bright, burning ball of energy behind them is me. They must learn to get out of my way...or die. GET OUT OF MY WAY! Fuck...get outta my way...please...pleeeease...get out of my way."

The man with all his pleading, cursing and angst still remains stuck in traffic. For all his rush. For all of his drama. For all his boiling blood. He remains in traffic. All he wants is some more beer. That is all.

"Just a few more drops. A sixer is not enough. My thirst never seems quenched."

This scene is repeated over and over throughout the cities of our world. Impatient people in cars. Stuck and angry. Angry for whatever reason. Some reasons small, some reasons big....and some are just on beer runs.

The Trap

Dear editor,

      I do not know why I am writing you. The first time it happened it was very early in the morning. I was in my room at the computer, doing whatever it is a lone male does at such a time. Over all the high-pitched noise coming from my speakers, I heard a bang and crash coming from my living room. Then I heard footsteps in and around the kitchen area. Could have been a ghost, but that would not have alarmed me so. Because of this I pulled up my boxers, ripped the computer cords from the wall and jettisoned myself out of my opened window. I was not scared. Like I said, alarmed. (I don't usually have fear like most and this was a mixture of fight-or-flight syndrome and entertainment). I circled around to the front door where somebody or something had entered. Before going in I turned the power off at the breaker box. Once in I could hear it in my room. I borrowed a knife from the kitchen. This was before I rid my house of carpet (you learn as you go on these things). It was very dark and the thing was making a lot of noise. It just knocked over my guitar. I know where things are by memory. I gained surprise on it. I swung my knife into the shadowy thing. I plunged my metal into it. It cursed and pleaded "Fuck, I'm not armed!" It was a man! I slashed at the outline of his throat. I put my full force into it! All the man did now was run and crash around gurgling and gasping. I felt a warm liquid over my hands and a smell of copper. I licked my knife clean.

That was some time ago and what remains of the man is nothing. I ripped out my carpet and acid treated my concrete floors. I got a loan. Bought a bunch of bright and shiny toys for yard décor: speedboat and an RV. Moved my work office into my house. Upgraded my automobile and hired a guy to drive my car away at 8:30 a.m. and bring it back at 5:30 p.m. Monday through Friday. I started a garden in the backyard and now I make my own fertilizer. I made a homemade crusher to pulverize things. Bought two huge freezers for meat. I may go broke but I have an obedience to my taste!

Blood tastes like copper. (I have liked mine but after licking that blade I prefer others).

Eyeballs taste like melted beef fat, wrapped in a gummy gelatinous balloon. I cook everything.

Human meat? Like veal. So much so I do not think one could discern the difference!

Liver has a strong flavor, especially if that person drank much. I recommend thin strips breaded and fried.

Tongue? Grilled.

Testicles? Breaded, fried.

Breasts? Hmmmmm...no women have broken into my place yet.

As you can probably tell by now, my palate has strayed from societal norms. Because of this, I am helping society by getting rid of certain types of human blight. I am judge, jury, and chef! It is easy to pick out the sordid souls that meet their end in my confines. The one tried-and-true method is this. If they are found in my dwellings while I am "away" that is all I need. THE GAVEL HAS LANDED! Grab a beer and fire up the grill! You see, my place is specially designed. It has certain false floors, rooms that emit certain gases, doors that cannot be opened from the inside. Behind the drywall, steel plates and sound proofing, and it looks rather bare inside. (I'm not very materialistic as it turns out). The windows are normal, but when you come in from out, there is probably a ten foot drop. All of this construction of course was done discreetly and has taken no small amount of my time.

Seeing all of my expensive frivolities, all sorts of folks get stuck in here, none of them honest people like you or me. Fat, skinny, tall, small, delicious and badly seasoned (that last part is almost always my fault). All are thieves, none are killers, and I have definitely had no cannibals. Most are on methamphetamines, and after consuming some of these types I have a hard time sleeping. Maybe it's my conscience? I don't know. For whatever reason nobody really comes looking for these people...here anyway. I guess my place would seem a kind of strange place for a stranger to be? It's been ten years now that I have been doing this and not one soul has come in search of one of my meals. My pulse no longer races at a knock on the door or ding of my bell. I am very comfortable in my trap.

If by chance you are driving down a street in a very ordinary suburban track and you come across a house with a boat on one side of the yard and a motor home on the other, accompanied by a fancy sports car...stop on by and come on in. You are invited to come inside...BUT ONLY IF THAT CAR IS NOT THERE!

~Anonymous~

The Job

"At three months you get the option of, basically, never actually working again."

"Here at Aid Rite you will never 'watch the clock' and you will NEVER have a bad day at work!"

"Life is waiting for you outside of Aid Rite!"

"Aid Rite, never take work home with you!"

"Aid Rite, where you will be your own dog!"

The boxes keep coming non-stop. There is a constant motor hum and an insistent clickity-clack that the boxes make when they move from the conveyer belt to the rolling pins. My box cutter makes a shish-shish-shish-shish sound as I rotate the box. When a box hits the exit conveyor belt it makes vvvhhheeesshhh sound until the box catches up with the belt speed. The workers on both my left and right are faster, but they don't care about my speed. The boxes keep coming...hummm, clickity-clack, shish-shish-shish-shish, vvvhhheeesshhh...they keep moving. There is almost no sound. The seconds tick by slowly. My productivity sheet says I cut 30,000 boxes daily. My manager wants 50,000 cut daily and wants me to plug in when my option is given tomorrow. I am nervous.

They say when one plugs in that it goes black for a moment, like a three-second blink, and that's it. That some days, after being plugged, you'll find cuts on your hands or that some of your muscles are sore but that's it. Your day of work is completed in as long as it takes to finish a three-second blink. There are other options, like being plugged and watching your favorite movies all shift, but most opt to take the three-second nap. Coworkers tell me it's great. They say that it's like being on vacation for a living. There are no educational programs while plugged in. When you're off of work, it's always off so you can spend time with all your family and friends. Aid Rite is lobbying for lowering the legal starting age for a worker to thirteen and also wants folks who are good at video games. One of their sayings is, "Dexterity leads to prosperity." And many of my co-workers believe it. Plugged workers get pay increases with time and also anytime they are updated. Being updated is having a download put into a bio-drive that has grown into a worker's brain. It programs a plugged worker to cut faster and, in down time, relieve muscle soreness. When Aid Rite first started the program twenty years ago, workers would become crippled with arthritis because plugged people only used one side or the other, and muscle build up would inversely affect the body as a whole. At that time workers would only have one job that they could be programmed to do and they would not switch from one day to the next performing their onus with different sides of the body. That has changed; all programs are now ambidextrous. New programs are coming out all the time. Unfortunately the bio-drive updates that pay best are those that also expand the bio-drive a little bit, and because of this there is less room in the cranial cavity. However, these are the updates that pay BIG and only a small change in personality can be detected by those who really know a worker.

"At Aid Rite, a little bit can make you ZIP, ZIP, ZIP all the way to the bank!" Aid Rite gives special incentives to families that become Aid Rite employees too. Like getting in free to the Aid Rite amusement park.

"At Aid Rite we are all one and one for all!"

So many of my friends and family are now plugged that I still do not know why I am a nervous wreck this morning. I should be calm. It doesn't look so bad. Also, I know what I'm going to say. I'm going to decline their offer. My uncle became a manager for higher pay. Since then he never gets any of my jokes. My mom too. She use to love to paint. I love writing classical music. My brother camps all the time, but he can only go on weekends and complains that it's a lot of work constantly packing up and putting up and tearing down camp for one night. None of them get holidays off. My niece has seen almost every movie known to man, but can only recall bits and pieces of them. My life is boring, I hate cutting boxes and I hate working. I wish I could write my music all of the time.

"Here at Aid Rite you can write your music ALL of the time!"

I met my manager once, while at a bar, before he became a manager. He had just been hired and he kept waxing on about how he had a great disdain for corporations and how they seemed to be taking over the world. His discourse was thought-provoking. I saw him again, after he became a manager at Aid Rite, while in the restroom of a Hooters and he just kept on talking about "Dem tit tays" and pointing and laughing while he peed all over the toilet paper roll. This thing was going to interview me the very next day!

"So Mr. Page you have been with Aid Rite now for about three months. What impressions do you have of our company? You know I really prefer to call it a family." I could tell he was different. Different from the guy who hated corporations. Different from the buffoon peeing on the toilet roll. He was being eloquent in a scripted sort of way. Like playing a programmed computer in a game of verbal chess. Though this program did not respond to you other than saying "I see" to your what, when, how, and why questions. "Of course by now you have heard of our plug-in option program called Freedom, Mr. Page? It is a splendid way to start your new career with our Aid Rite family. I myself have taken the plunge into this brave new world of happiness! Happiness, Mr. Page, complete and unhindered happiness with almost no strings attached."

"Mr. Page you still seem to have doubts about whether you could succeed in our family. Rest assured, I know you would be great!"

"I must also remind you that those that do not join our wonderful Freedom program do not usually reap the financial rewards of those who do. Also, our statistics show that they usually do not last more than four months here at Aid Rite. And, Mr. Page, we have a no rehire policy."

"I see you are still unsure of whether you want to be a part of the Freedom program. Perhaps you would like to see our corporate movie in our very own company theatre?"

"Swell, Mr. Page, just perfect!"

(A flash of white light and a high pitch whine)

4.3.2.1…4.3.2.1…4.3.2.1. Here at Aid Rite we are all fami1ly. That's right, family. One large family where all are one and one are all. That's all. We don't work to1gether, we plug-in togeth1er and move as one. We go on family outings together. Sometimes we even go to the Aid Rite amusement park and garden and have fun, fun, fun. We are all one and one are all. 1. It will seem that all you do is play, play, play, Mr.Page. There is no time to work at Aid Rite. 1. There is no time to worry and only time for hobbies. 1. And music Mr. Page, MUSIC! Music that was 1 written by YOU. That you can share with your Aid Rite family. All are 1 and on1e are al1. We are 1one and we bleed as 1. Our heart beats   as one.11111111111111111111111111111111111111111111

1111111111111111111
11111111111111111111111111111111111111111111111
111111111111111111111111111111
11111111111111111111111111111111111111111111111
1111111111111111111111111111111. AID RITE1111IIIIIIIISSSSSSSS11111111FREEDOM1111111111FREE DOM IS AID RITE1111111111111111FREEDUMB11111111111111111111 1111ONE11IS11ALL11AND11ALL11ARE11ONE. (Another flash of bright white light and a high pitch whine) 1.2.3.4...1.2.3.4...1.2.3.4.

The End

I saw a flash of light and heard a high pitch whine. I don't even remember the movie. It seemed like a three-second blink. When I looked at my watch it was eight hours later. I felt normal, but I was tired, almost like I had been cutting boxes all day except like I had cut more than I ever had before. My workmates were congratulating me for joining the Aid Rite family and wanted to buy me drinks at the Aid Rite bar. I don't remember signing anything. Now when I go to work it only seems like a three-second blink. I write my music all the time and never work. I do seem to cut my hair and shave all the time and it seems as if my birthday comes four times a year, which is fine by me. My old friends and family don't seem to get my jokes anymore or like the songs I have written after I became a manager at Aid Rite but my Aid Rite family can't get enough of them!

It's funny. I don't remember being plugged-in. I don't know why I was nervous that day at my option interview, my worries back then seem so small. I don't have any worries now that I have my Aid Rite family. That thought now makes me very warm inside. I will always have my Aid Rite family! I love my Aid Rite family!

"Here at Aid Rite. Aid Rite is LOVE!"

www.ingramcontent.com/pod-product-compliance
Lightning Source LLC
Chambersburg PA
CBHW020547130626
46552CB00007B/2794